Ingrid Mennen was inspired to write *One Round Moon and a Star for Me*
when her youngest daughter Frieda asked her the question,
"Mama, are you really my mama too?" Later, after hearing about the family,
customs and life of a Lesotho friend, Ingrid decided to weave this question
into a story about a young boy's celebration of life in the expansive
countryside of Lesotho in southern Africa.

Niki Daly's illustrations were planned in his studio in the city of Cape Town.
He says, "After I sketched the initial drawings from my imagination,
I travelled to Lesotho and found all the scenes and people I had drawn
back home. Somehow I must have travelled there in thought while
sitting at my drawing board."

Both Ingrid and Niki live in South Africa. Niki's previous
books for Frances Lincoln include *Not So Fast, Songololo,*
Once Upon a Time and the Jamela series.

ONE ROUND MOON

and a star for me

ONE ROUND MOON

and a star for me

STORY BY

Ingrid Mennen

& ILLUSTRATIONS BY

Niki Daly

FRANCES LINCOLN CHILDREN'S BOOKS

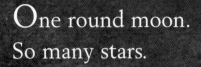

One round moon.
So many stars.

A falling star, Mama!
Look how Papa catches it in his warm brown blanket.
See how it slips into his silver milk bucket.
"A star for a new baby," says Mama.

Now, Moon, please go! Go to your home.
Go sleep in your hut. Roll up night.
Look how Sun is chasing Moon, Mama.
Big round moon, back to her empty hut.

Ah! There! One round sun!
Hurry through the grass – make it gold.
Run over the hill, past Papa's herd.

Come, Sun, here! Come warm our home.
For there's a brand-new baby in our hut today.

Mamkhulu – my aunty – lifts me high. I stick two stalks of sun-yellow grass in the roof, above the door. Mamkhulu says, "Now the men will come in only when the inkaba cord falls from the baby's belly."

Three makoties – three young girls – bring water
for the baby, balancing buckets on their heads.

Sis Beauty brings a new cake of soap she has saved for so long. Sis Anna brings a little paraffin lamp made from a tin and a piece of wick-cloth to light for the baby.

Gogo – our grandmother – and her friends
bring fresh cow dung for a new floor.

Inside, Mama sings a tula-tula hush-hush song
to the baby.

And then Papa comes. He leaves his silver bucket, brimming with milk, at the door and kneels to look at the baby's two tiny hands.

"They look like my hands," he says.

He looks at the baby's tiny round ears.

"Mama's ears."

He unwraps the blanket, and there are two small feet with ten tiny toes.

"They will walk well." Papa nods.

"I'm the baby's father," says Papa with a smile.

We walk to the other men, but my heart
feels dark, like a night with no moon.
At last I ask, "Papa, are you really
my papa too?"

He takes my hands and puts them next to his.
"See," he says. "I am really your papa too."
He looks me close in the eye. "Your eyes are
like Mama's eyes. You are your papa's child
and you are your mama's child."

He puts his arms around me and says,
"Tonight, when the moon is big and round
and the stars light up God's great sky,
I'll show you, there is also a star for you."

One round moon.

And a star for me.

For Joyce, who shares her life with me – I.M.
For Laura Cecil, my friend and agent – N.D.

This edition published in 2004 by Frances Lincoln Children's Books,
4 Torriano Mews, Torriano Ave, London NW5 2RZ

First published by Orchard Books, New York in 1994
First published in the United Kingdom in 1994
by The Bodley Head Children's Books

British Library Cataloguing in Publication Data available on request

1-84507-024-0 (HB)
1-84507-025-9 (PB)

Printed in China

1 3 5 7 9 8 6 4 2

OTHER TITLES WRITTEN AND ILLUSTRATED BY NIKI DALY AVAILABLE FROM FRANCES LINCOLN

NOT SO FAST, SONGOLOLO

Gogo is old, but her face shines like new shoes. "I must do
my shopping in the city," she says. "Yu! Those mad cars!"
Her grandson Shepherd likes taking his time, so he's perfect
to help Gogo, and as they weave their way through the
colourful bustle of the African city, Shepherd is given a treat
that will put a new spring in his step.
ISBN 0-7112-1765-3

JAMELA'S DRESS

When Mama asks Jamela to keep an eye on her new dress material
as it hangs out to dry, Jamela can't resist wrapping it around herself
and dancing down the road, proud as a peacock ... Then things
go wrong, and Mama is very sad indeed, but guess who ends up with
the biggest smile? KWELA JAMELA AFRICAN QUEEN, that's who!
ISBN 0-7112-1449-2

ONCE UPON A TIME

When Sarie's teacher says, "Children, take out your reading books,"
a sick feeling grips Sarie. The words trip up her tongue and she
stutters and stammers, making the children in the back row giggle.
But Ou Missus, the old lady living over the veld, is sympathetic.
One Sunday, Sarie comes across an old copy of Cinderella
and begs Ou Missus to read it to her. Ou Missus says,
"No – we will read it together."
ISBN 0-7112-1993-1

Frances Lincoln titles are available from all good bookshops.
You can also buy books and find out more about your favourite titles,
authors and illustrators on our website: www.franceslincoln.com